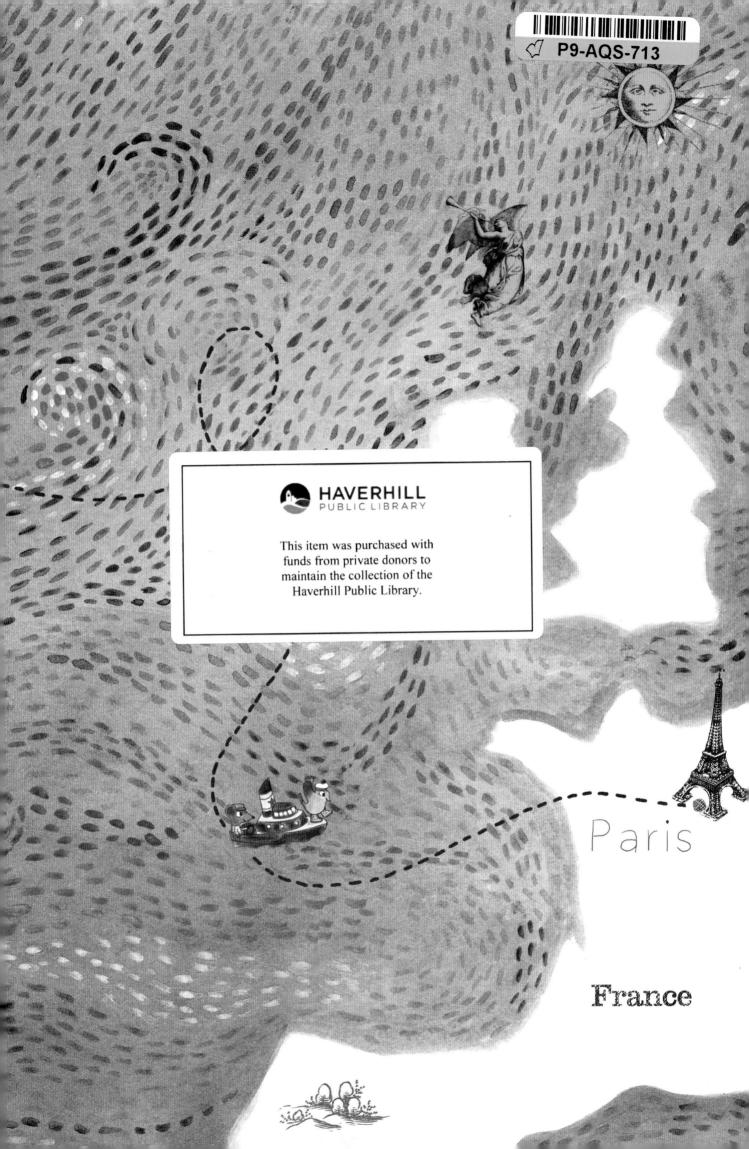

Paris

France

Emma
in Paris

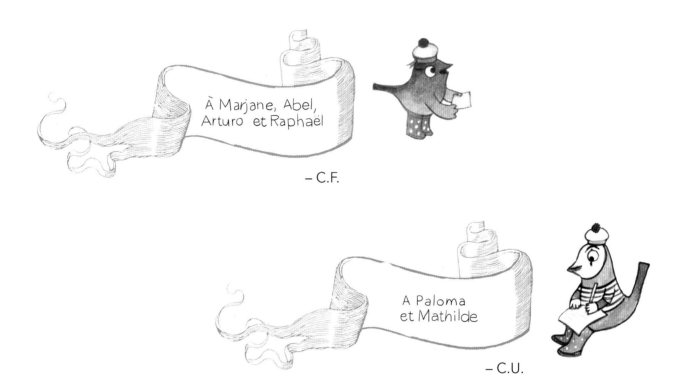

À Marjane, Abel,
Arturo et Raphaël

– C.F.

A Paloma
et Mathilde

– C.U.

www.enchantedlion.com

First American edition published in 2013 by Enchanted Lion Books,
351 Van Brunt Street, Brooklyn, NY 11231
Printed on 157 gsm Huaxia Sun Matt Art Paper
Text and illustrations copyright © 2013 by Claire Frossard
Photographs copyright © 2013 by Christophe Urbain
English-language edition copyright © 2013 by Enchanted Lion Books
All rights reserved under International and Pan-American Copyright Conventions
A CIP record is on file with the Library of Congress
ISBN: 978-1-59270-139-1
Printed and bound in September 2013 by South China Printing Company

The sparrow Emma Moineau was born and
raised in New York City's Central Park.
She now has crossed the Atlantic Ocean to visit Paris
and to meet her French cousin, Amélie Moineau.

Emma
in Paris

Written and illustrated
by Claire Frossard

Photographs
by Christophe Urbain

ENCHANTED LION BOOKS
NEW YORK

The air is sweet. It's summer and Emma is enjoying a fresh croissant on the banks of the Seine. She has just arrived in Paris, with an address in her pocket: *125 rue des Abbesses, Montmartre.* This is where her cousin Amélie lives.

Emma already knows some French:
"bonjour," "merci," and "au revoir."*
Proud of her new abilities, Emma greets a woman with "Bonjour!"
Then, in English, she explains that she is looking for her cousin's house.
The elegant woman smiles, but shakes her head. She's sorry.
She doesn't speak any English.

*Hello, thank you, and goodbye.

Emma approaches a couple of crows to ask for directions.
Before she can even open her beak, they say,
"**Non, merci**"* and hurry away. Emma is a little surprised
by their response, but bravely continues to look
for someone who will help her.

*No, thank you.

Non, merci.

In a passageway off the Faubourg
Saint-Martin, Emma sees a kindly
old mouse sitting on a bench.
She shows him the slip of paper
with the address.

"**Oh là là,**"* he mutters. "My eyes
aren't good enough to read that!"

Emma tries to explain where she
wants to go, but the old mouse
doesn't seem to hear a word she says.

*Oh, dear.

*What?

Emma passes a bookseller's stand and decides to stop. She has only a few cents left. Just enough, it turns out, to buy a French-English dictionary. Now she can really begin to practice her French, which she does out loud, repeating her words over and over again.

Emma doesn't seem to be having any luck. On the lawn of the
Palais Royal, everybody is so busy that no one pays any attention to her.

PELOUSE
INTERDITE

She is beginning to feel like giving up when she sees a twenty-sous bill slip from the pocket of a little white cat who is just passing by. Emma picks it up, hesitating. After all, she's hungry and has no money left.

But Emma hesitates only for a moment. Then she sets off after the cat to return his money to him. She moves swiftly and catches up with him.

"Merci, mademoiselle,"* says the cat. Emma nods shyly and begins to ask for directions in English.

*Thank you, young lady.

"I will help you," says the cat. "But first, to thank you for your honesty, I would like to invite you to eat a little something with me." Once again Emma hesitates, but only for a moment. She is so hungry and the cat seems so kind that she can't refuse.

A **croque-monsieur*** later, Edouard
the cat and Emma almost seem able
to understand each other.

Emma is still a little on her guard.
After all, she's only a little sparrow
and needs to beware of cats! But
Edouard is gentle, and since he's
never left Paris, he's amazed by her
adventures and listens to her stories
of New York with dreams in his eyes.

*A grilled ham and cheese sandwich.

They talk until evening. Then Edouard accompanies
Emma to the Abesses metro station and tells her how
to find her cousin Amélie.

"Don't forget," says Edouard, "tomorrow is
Bastille Day*. I am hosting a ball at the Chemin Vert
metro station, so please come with your cousin!"

"I will!" Emma replies. "I promise."

*Bastille Day is the name given in English-speaking countries to the French
National Day, which is celebrated on July 14th.

As she stands in front of Amélie's door, Emma feels happy, anxious, and amazed, all at the same time. She knocks timidly, and Amélie opens the door. "Emma!" Amélie exclaims. "I'm so happy to see you! Uncle Bob told me you were in Paris. I've been waiting for you!"

The two sparrows chatter away for hours. Amélie can speak a bit of English, and Emma feels comfortable trying out her French with her cousin. They talk about Emma's ocean crossing and about her first impressions of Paris. Amélie also tells Emma about her life as a performer in a street circus and her trips to Rome, London and Venice. Emma is captivated! There is still so much for her to discover.

The next day, after her fire-eating performance in the Tuileries Garden, Amélie tells Emma that she's been looking for a circus partner, and she asks Emma to join her act.

"I'll teach you how to juggle, walk on a wire, mime, and eat fire!"
Emma is overjoyed!
"Let's celebrate!"
They decide to begin by going to Edouard's Bastille Day party.

At first, Emma and Amélie are a little frightened. There are so many cats!

But Edouard welcomes them and reassures them.

"Do not worry," he says. "You are my guests! Just dance and enjoy the party!"

The cats eye the plump sparrows with appetite, but there are so many other good things to eat—sweet milk pudding, fish stew, and berry bread, to name just a few—that they soon lose interest in the birds.

This is Emma's first ball, and they dance happily till dawn.

The first few months pass quickly. Emma is now very busy because she and Amélie are performing their show all over the city.

On Mondays, they juggle at Place des Vosges.

On Tuesdays, they walk the tightrope on the Pont-Neuf,
one of the many bridges that cross the Seine River.

On Wednesday evenings,
they perform as clowns for the tourists
in front of Notre-Dame Cathedral.

On Thursdays, their day off, Emma always meets Edouard for an ice cream. Now it's Emma who orders, almost without an accent. **"Bonjour, deux sorbets citron-cassis, s'il vous plait!"***

*Hello, two blueberry-lemon sorbets, please!

On Fridays, after performing a mime show in the Tuileries, Emma and Amélie like to relax. They have a snack, and often write a letter to Emma's parents and Uncle Bob.

Dear Mom and Dad, dear Aunt and Uncle, dear Uncle Bob,
We have become the best of friends ever! We are now putting
on a show together that is becoming very popular!
Hugs & Kisses,
A & E

On Saturdays, with some other acrobats, they perform their favorite act, which they call "The Perilous Tower."

On Sundays, they do all sorts of things.
Sometimes they prepare a big lunch for friends.
Occasionally they visit a museum.
Often they stay home to read, eat cake and sleep.
They also like to dream about faraway places
and the adventures that await them.

On one very special Sunday, they meet on the Pont des Arts to attach a lock engraved with their names. Like all of the other friends that have placed locks here, they do so to seal their friendship forever.

MONUMENTAL
'ETRANGER DANS PARIS

Croix de la Bretonnerie - Paris

CORRESPONDS ⊙ STATION — Chemin de fer Métropolitain

Imp. Crété, Corbeil-Essonnes (S.-et-O.).

Etats-Unis

New-York